ALPHY DAVID

HIDDEN DEEP

ALPHY SCHOOL

Alphy David

HIDDEN DEEP

ALPHY BOOKS

Alphy School, Senekowitschgasse 8/5/16, Wien 1220, Austria

First printing edition 2022.

ISBN: 978-3-9505216-0-3 (Paperback)

ISBN: 978-3-9505216-1-0 (E-Book)

Any references to historical events, real people, or real places are used fictitiously. Names, characters, and places are products of the author's imagination.

Book design by David Vundi.

Alphy School

www.alphyschool.org

To

my little sister,

Xenia Anoushka

1

Springville, Utah
December 1953

Jack wrapped his woollen scarf tightly around his neck so that it concealed the lower half of his face. One of his hands was dragging a suitcase down a rough stone paved road, and the other was stuffed deep into his pocket. Jack looked down, focusing only on his steps and not on his destination.

"Careful now, dear," Jack's Aunt Felicity said, her voice full of fake kindness, "Are you sure you want to carry that suitcase, Jack? Your uncle can do that for you."

Jack shook his head and kept walking.

"Doesn't the blasted boy know how to talk?" his Uncle Daniel asked, rubbing his frozen hands together.

"Apparently not," Felicity said. She narrowed her eyes at Jack and moved along.

Jack looked up briefly, looking at the snow-covered street. There were small shops on either side of the street: bakeries, restaurants, and other places of interest. Jack looked down again and trudged along in the snow. Suddenly, he heard something. He closed his eyes and listened through the sounds of the street.

Keys were being pressed; strings were being played. The sound of music drifted into Jack's ears and made its way to his heart.

Debussy's Violin Sonata in G Minor, Jack thought, *One of my favourites.*

He walked forward, and his eyes darted around, searching for where the music came from. They finally rested on a small store tucked in between a bakery and a bookstore.

Anna's Place

Jack stared at the store and committed it to his memory. He wasn't watching where he was going. It all happened quite quickly. One second,

Jack was walking, and the next, he was sprawled on the pavement.

"I'm sorry! I'm sorry!" cried a sweet voice, "I didn't see you there!"

Jack didn't hear those last words. His scarf had fallen off, and his face was exposed. He looked around for his scarf but couldn't find it. He turned to his left, to hide that side of his face. Jack glanced up and saw a girl staring at him. She took his arm and helped him up. She picked up his scarf (which he had been lying on) and handed it to him. Then, she looked directly at his face.

Jack's ears were hot. He breathed heavily and refused to look at her. He didn't want to see the look of horror on the girl's face. He didn't want to see her leave abruptly. To his surprise, the girl remained standing and staring at him, until he was forced to look into her eyes.

What was this?

The girl was *smiling* at him! She had dark eyes and thick eyelashes. Her black hair was braided into two French braids, and she had a beautiful, strange smile. Jack could tell immediately what type of person she was just from her smile.

Jack's hand instinctively touched his face, where a long scar traced down his left cheek. One could see the stitches that were sewn on his cheek. They started from Jack's ear and went under his chin. Most people were horrified by it. They avoided him as though he was some sort of monster.

This girl, however, didn't seem to have a problem with it.

"I'm sorry." she repeated. She was carrying a basket filled with fruit.

"T-that's alright." Jack's voice cracked, and he blushed.

He looked around for his aunt and uncle. Daniel was waiting for him at the end of the street, tapping his foot impatiently. Jack gave the girl a short smile and hurried to Daniel. Then, they started walking again. The street soon became steep, and Jack struggled to keep up. They stopped in front of two tall wooden doors. There were hedges as tall as the doors on both sides, covering the place that lay behind it.

Daniel opened the door, and they all walked inside. Jack was unable to stop himself from gasping. There was a large yard with trees surrounding it. A fountain stood in the middle of it and the gravel path Jack was standing on split into two, curving around the fountain and joining together once again. It led to a white mansion. Snow glittered on the roof and the path.

There was a single pair of footprints in the snow. Jack walked carefully in each print, not wanting to disturb the snow. The tracks reminded him of music notes because of their even pacing and size. Jack smiled at the thought of it.

"Aren't you a bit old for that?" Felicity asked, walking carelessly through the snow.

Jack did not answer. He followed her to the front door.

Daniel knocked.

As they waited for someone to open the door, Jack noticed a silver certificate that hung on the wall.

Dr.Thomas Willows, PhD., M.Phil., M.Ed.

Jack felt a burst of anger inside of him. *This* was the stranger he was being left with. He wanted to tear the certificate off the wall and smash it to pieces. Thomas Willows was a good friend of Daniel and Felicity.

Any friend of theirs was his enemy.

2

The door was opened by a man wearing a butler's outfit. He looked at all three of them for a moment and then smiled.

"Mr and Mrs Stanley!" he exclaimed, "Welcome! Please come inside."

He took their wet coats and hung them out to dry. Jack examined the entrance hall. A long red carpet led to an imperial staircase. There were a few rooms on both sides of the hall.

"Please follow me. I am Rogers, Mr Willows' butler. He has been expecting you." Rogers said and led them up the staircase and down a long corridor. At the end of it was a set of wooden doors. Rogers knocked.

"Come in." grunted a voice.

They walked into a beautiful room filled with paintings. The room was bathed in sunlight from the many windows. A glass table was set at the centre of the room. A man in a plaid suit and matching pants was sitting in one of the several armchairs. He had dark hair and dramatic brown eyes. Jack glanced at him for a second.

Was the man *crying*?

Jack averted his gaze as the man stood.

"Daniel, Felicity," he said, walking towards them. He spoke elegantly, "So good to see you again. It's been a long time."

"Yes, it has, Thomas." Daniel said and shook his hand.

Jack looked down so that Thomas Willows wouldn't be able to see his face. He tried to hide behind Felicity. Thomas spotted him anyway.

"And this must be young Jack." he said.

Jack looked up at Thomas, who was not smiling. Any sign of tears was gone.

"Nice to meet you, sir," Jack whispered, shaking his hand.

Thomas nodded at him.

"We can't thank you enough for this, Thomas." Felicity said. "Daniel and I have been looking forward to this trip. We didn't want to drag Jack around boring him to death."

Jack looked away so that no one would see him roll his eyes. Rogers the butler, who was standing at the door, chuckled softly.

"Not at all." Thomas replied, "It-it's the least I can do."

There was a moment of silence. Jack could feel the tension between his uncle and aunt and Thomas.

Thomas cleared his throat, "Well, our cook has prepared a wonderful supper. You will stay, won't you?"

"Thank you, old friend, but we must get going," Daniel said. "Our train leaves soon."

All of them walked back to the entrance hall, where Rogers helped Felicity and Daniel with their coats. Daniel patted Jack on the head, and Felicity leaned down and kissed him on the cheek. Jack felt an unexpected tug on his heart, and tears pricked his eyes.

"Be good now, dear." Felicity said, "We'll be back before you know it."

Please don't leave me. Jack wanted to say, but his voice wouldn't work.

Daniel and Felicity thanked Thomas once again, and then, they were gone. Jack stood next to Thomas, not knowing what to do.

"Rogers, gather the others to the Dining Hall, will you?" Thomas said. Rogers went to do his bidding.

The others? Jack wondered.

Thomas put a hand on Jack's shoulder and led him down another corridor, "Now, Jack, I would like you to meet the other servants, then I will give you a brief tour of the house."

Jack nodded. They entered the Dining Hall. A long table for perhaps twelve people stood at the centre. This room was also filled with big windows and paintings. Soon, three people filed into the room with Rogers and stood in front of Jack and Thomas.

"This is Marta, the cook." Thomas said, gesturing to the middle-aged woman with her hair in a tight knot. She smiled at Jack.

"Theo, the gardener." A handsome young man with blond hair and strong arms. "Ansley the housekeeper," A beautiful young lady winked at

Jack, "And you've already met Rogers, Marta's husband."

Thomas frowned and looked around, as though he was forgetting something.

"Ansley, where's Elodie?" he asked.

"I sent her out to get groceries for me." Ansley replied, "She should be back any-"

There was the slam of a door and someone yelling, "I'm here! I'm here!"

Jack heard the sound of running, and suddenly someone bumped into Thomas.

"And here is Elodie," Thomas muttered, "here for small jobs but mostly for bumping into any living soul she can find."

Elodie grinned, and Jack recognized her as the girl he met in the market. She looked like a smaller version of Ansley. Jack smiled at her.

"If you ever need anything, just ask one of them." Thomas told him.

After that, Thomas showed Jack the library ("The biggest one in town."), the study ("My private space, and will not be entered without permission."), the front and back yard ("Perfectly catered."), and the forest behind the backyard ("You will under no circumstances enter it.")

The tour was finished at last, and Jack could barely stand.

"I suppose I'll show you to your room now."

Thomas led Jack to the second floor and into a large bedroom with a four-poster bed, an oak wardrobe, and a small desk and dresser. The wallpaper was gold, casting a soft glow on the room.

"Do you like it?" Thomas asked.

Jack nodded.

"Talk, boy," Thomas said, "I asked you a question. Do you like it?"

"Y-yes sir, I do," Jack stammered.

"From now on, you will call me Uncle Thomas. You better learn to speak up if you want to live here." Thomas said roughly. "You already look repulsive with that scar of yours. If you're quiet as well, people will mistake you for an illiterate troll."

With that, Thomas turned on his heel and left.

Jack's ears burned, he blinked back tears and furiously started unpacking. Once he was done, he slammed the suitcase shut and shoved it under his bed. Jack traced a finger along his scar and looked at his reflection in the mirror above the dresser. The word Thomas had said kept echoing in his head.

Repulsive.

3

Supper was a quiet, awkward affair. Thomas asked Jack short questions to which he gave short answers. Jack went to bed early, curling up in the unfamiliar covers. It took him a while to remember where he was when he awoke. Jack looked out the window and saw thick snowflakes falling. Then, there was a knock on the door.

"Come in." Jack said.

The door was opened by Ansley.

"Good morning, master Jack." Ansley greeted with a smile, "I'm Ansley, in case you don't remember."

Jack smiled shyly back at her.

"I've come to call you down for breakfast."

"Oh, I'll be down soon."

Jack dressed quickly and stepped outside his bedroom. Ansley was waiting for him.

"Breakfast is informal here." Ansley explained as they walked to the Dining Hall. "You don't have to dress up that much."

She gestured to what Jack was wearing. He nodded. They walked into the Dining Hall. A single plate was set next to a several platters of food. Jack's heart sank, it all looked very small and lonely.

"You can always come sit with us if you don't prefer eating alone." Ansley said, seeing his pained face. "It's not as fancy as all this, but it *is* fun."

"I don't mind." Jack said.

Ansley led him to the room across from the Dining Hall. The Kitchen. To one side of the room were a stove and cupboards. The other side had a wooden dining table where Marta, Rogers, Theo, and Elodie were sitting. Ansley cleared her throat, "We have a recruit, crew." Ansley said. "Theo, get him a chair."

"Aye, aye, captain," said Theo, saluting her.

Elodie giggled. Marta got up and set a plate in front of Jack. It was filled with food. Jack eyed it worriedly, wondering how he would finish it all.

"Don't worry, master Jack." laughed Theo, "There's a stray dog that comes here every day. We give him all our leftovers."

Jack smiled and took a bite of eggs. His eyes fluttered, and he couldn't suppress a sigh.

"Good, isn't it? Marta makes the best food in town." Ansley complimented. Marta flushed with pride.

"Um, excuse me, but is it okay that I'm sitting here when Mr Willows is eating alone?" Jack asked.

"Mr Willows already left for work, master Jack." Marta said, "More eggs?"

"Thank you," Jack replied, "and all of you can call me Jack."

Breakfast was soon finished, and everyone cleared the table while Jack sat, unsure of what was expected of him. He then saw a pair of brown eyes intently staring at him.

"I'm Elodie." she said, sticking out her arm.

"I know, I mean, hi." Jack blushed and shook her hand.

"I have to go to town." Elodie told Jack, "Want to come?"

"Um, sure."

Elodie grinned and dragged Jack to the entrance hall. They put on their coats and laced up their boots. Jack tied his scarf tightly around his neck. He and Elodie walked out into the white yard. Once again, Jack walked in Elodie's footsteps so as not to disturb the snow. Elodie was carrying a basket, and snowflakes fell on her uncovered head.

She reminded Jack much of Little Red Riding Hood, with her braided hair and the skip in her step.

"Aren't you uncomfortable with that scarf?" Elodie asked.

Jack shook his head, "I've gotten used to it."

"What about in the summer? How do you uh, cover yourself then?" Elodie asked, not wanting to sound rude.

"I don't go out much in summer." Jack told her, "I just stay in my uncle's backyard."

Elodie looked at him for a while, "You know, nobody will mind if you have that scar. Of course, people will stare, but who really cares."

Jack forced himself not to roll his eyes. What did *she* know?

Elodie was quiet for some time, "Do you mind me asking, what happened to your parents? Why do you live with your aunt and uncle?"

Jack sighed, "My parents died when I was young. I don't know how; nobody will tell me. I've never even seen their graves. That's why I live with my aunt and uncle."

"Oh, I'm sorry."

"So, where are we going?" asked Jack, determined to not start off on the wrong foot.

"To buy strawberry tarts from The Peters Bakery." Elodie replied. "Mr Willows developed a taste for them."

They walked for a while and then came across The Peters Bakery: a large bakery with a window display, filled with scrumptious-looking desserts. Elodie and Jack walked inside. The aroma of fresh bread and the heat hypnotised him. As they waited in line, Jack began to sweat. He scratched his neck uncomfortably. It was finally their turn.

"Elodie!" cried a plump man in an apron, "The usual?"

"Yup." said Elodie, smiling, "Thanks, Mr Peters. This is Jack."

"Mr Willows' new ward, huh?" Mr Peters said, narrowing his eyes at Jack, "Nice to meet you."

"Nice to meet you too, sir," Jack's muffled voice came from under his scarf.

As Mr Peters prepared Elodie's order, Jack noticed that he talked directly to Elodie and avoided Jack. He wondered how Mr Peters knew that he was Mr Willows' ward. Once he was done, Mr Peters handed Elodie a small box, she put it in her basket.

"Thank you, Mr Peters." she said, "Bye!"

They walked out of the store, and Jack breathed a sigh of relief. He turned to return to the mansion, but Elodie started going into the shop next door.

"Aren't we going back?" Jack asked.

"We can't come into town without visiting Tyler and Marie!" she replied.

Elodie looped her arm around Jack's and skipped forward. Jack looked closer at the shop next to the bakery.

Anna's Place. The music store! Jack decided it wasn't such a bad idea to go into another shop. He walked with Elodie to the entrance. The window display had two violins hung above a small diorama of an orchestra. The maestro held his arms high. They walked through the door, and the bell above it clang. There were only two others in the store.

Jack breathed in. The smell of wood filled the air. A phonograph was placed in the corner of the room, playing Beethoven's 6th Symphony. There were violins on the wall, accordions and flutes on shelves, a few cellos, and a grand piano on a small platform in the corner.

"Well, if it isn't my favourite customer!" said a man walking up to Elodie and Jack. He had laughing eyes and greying brown hair.

"Good morning, Tyler." Elodie greeted, smiling.

A woman came out from a room behind the counter carrying a box of paper. Although her face was old, she was still very good-looking.

"Hello, Elodie." she said, "What can we do for you today?" She set the box down and rested her elbows on the counter.

"Just came to say hi, Marie." Elodie said.

Marie looked over Elodie and saw Jack standing with his arms behind his back. A smile lit up her face, "And this must be Jack!" she exclaimed.

Jack looked up in surprise, "Yes, ma'am." he said, "How did you know?"

"Elodie's been babbling about you ever since she heard that you were coming." Tyler said, laughing, "I nearly lost my hearing."

"*Tyler*, I didn't do that." Elodie said trying not to let her embarrassment show.

"Of course, you didn't, Elodie." Tyler said, winking.

Jack smiled.

Elodie suddenly shoved the basket into Jack's hands and ran over to the piano. She opened the lid and poised her fingers over the keys. Then, Elodie played a short polka and grinned.

"Tyler is teaching me piano. I've been using this piano to practise." she told him.

"She's getting better, isn't she?" Marie said, "Do you play any instruments, Jack?"

Jack's face closed up, "Well, I used to."

Everyone waited.

"*What* instrument?" Elodie questioned.

"Violin." Jack muttered.

Tyler smiled, "I am a violinist myself. I make them as well."

"You must play for us sometime, Jack." Marie said.

Jack nodded and looked down; he shuffled his feet. Elodie noticed he was getting uncomfortable and decided to get going.

"We have to go." Elodie said, "Ansley will be expecting us. See you later."

"Feel free to stop by anytime." Tyler told them.

Elodie and Jack bid them farewell and stepped outside. Jack breathed in the icy air.

"What was that about?" Elodie asked.

"What?" Jack asked, with irritation.

"You started freaking out."

"It was just stuffy in there." Jack said shortly and walked ahead of her.

He felt awful. Elodie was being so nice to him, and here he was snapping at her. But Jack didn't want to admit the real reason he was afraid of Marie's question. He didn't want to scare the only person who didn't judge him. Thankfully, Elodie only frowned and followed him.

On the way back home, Jack saw a large building with boarded-up windows. The paint was peeling off and small piles of rubble were forming next to it.

"What's that?" Jack asked.

"That's just the old theatre." Elodie told him. "It's been shut down for years."

They walked back to the house in silence. Elodie led Jack to the back door which went to the kitchen. Marta greeted them at their arrival. She took the basket from Elodie and asked Jack if he wanted to help her bake. Jack agreed with a strained smile. He spent the rest of the day helping Marta in the kitchen and reading in his room. He tried to read in the library, but it seemed too big.

Thomas came home at around four and immediately disappeared into his study. Jack remained in his room, dawdling, and turning down

Elodie's offers to play. Dinner was, once again, quiet, and unpleasant. Jack couldn't wait to escape to his room. As he walked up the stairs, Jack heard Elodie and Ansley talking.

"I don't think he likes me very much, Ansley." he heard Elodie say.

"Why wouldn't he like you?" Ansley asked.

"He didn't want to play with me, no matter how many times I asked him. I even decorated his room."

"He's adjusting to a lot of new things," Elodie." Ansley told her, "Give him some time and I know he'll like you as soon as he gets to know you better.""

Jack had no doubt they were talking about him, and he sighed sadly. Elodie was badly in need of a friend. He thought about all this as he lay in bed. He was unable to sleep, nor stop his racing thoughts.

How would he survive this place for one year?

4

The next day, Jack slept in. Sunlight shone through the window, waking him. Jack rubbed his eyes and checked the clock on his dresser. 12:30.

Did I sleep in this late? Jack wondered as he dressed.

He stepped out into the corridor and was about to go downstairs when he heard music behind him. Jack spun around and followed the music through the house. Jack recognized the song as "Nearer My God to Thee", being played on the cello. The music led him upstairs to the second floor, where he had never been.

As Jack approached the door where the music came from, the song stopped abruptly, and he heard muffled shouting coming from the last door in the corridor. There was silence, and the song started again. Jack crept towards the door and peeked through the keyhole.

He saw Thomas standing impatiently, glaring at someone else in the room.

"Stop!" Thomas yelled and rubbed his head, "You cannot just simply play the song. Put some emotion into it!"

The music started again. Someone suddenly tapped Jack's shoulder, and he gasped.

"Sorry, Jack." Ansley said, "I didn't mean to scare you. I have a message for Mr Willows. You better hide here. No one is allowed in this room without Mr Willows' permission."

She gestured to the curtains drawn up in the corner.

"Thanks, Ansley." Jack said and dived behind the curtains.

Ansley knocked on the door.

"*What?*" Thomas roared.

Ansley cautiously opened the door, "Sorry to disturb you, sir, but Mr Parker from the lab is on the phone."

"Yes, yes." Thomas said, then he turned to the person playing the cello, "I will be back in fifteen minutes. *Practise.*"

With that, he and Ansley left. Jack looked through the curtains and saw a boy with hair the colour of straw frustratedly plucking on the cello strings. He looked to be about Jack's age. Jack slowly walked into the room. The boy raised his eyebrows and stopped playing. Jack took a moment to look around. He was in a music room filled with every kind instrument he had ever seen. Large windows took up one side of the room, and a wooden shelf, full of books, was on the other.

"Can I help you?" the boy asked.

"Sorry to interfere." said Jack, prying his eyes away from his surroundings, "But I think what Uncle Thomas means is that you should start the song like a calm ocean, and build up into a storm."

The boy looked at him, "I have no idea what you just said, nephew of Mr Willows."

"Actually, I'm not his nephew, I–"

"*Honestly,* it isn't that hard." Jack was interrupted by Elodie.

Both boys jumped.

Elodie strolled into the room and placed her hands on her hips, "Just start the song quietly and crescendo into it. Feel something while you're doing it, like anger or pain."

"And what do *you* know about music, Elodie?" the boy asked.

"More than you, you pathetic loser." said Elodie, walking over to the piano, "Just start, Carter."

The boy named Carter breathed in and began to play. After the first verse, Elodie joined him with the piano. Jack closed his eyes and listened. They were playing just the way he said to. Starting like a calm sea and building up to a raging ocean. Although they missed a few notes, it was beautiful. Once they finished, Jack clapped.

Carter grinned, "Hey, that sounded great!"

Jack nodded, "And you played with feeling. I'm Jack, by the way."

"Carter." The boys shook hands.

"Anyway, I wanted to ask if you want to play outside with me, Jack." Elodie said. "There is a fresh coat of snow."

"Can I come too?" Carter asked.

"Sure," Jack said.

"No," Elodie said at the same time, "You have a music lesson."

"Uncle Thomas teaches music?" Jack asked in wonder.

Elodie and Carter nodded.

"He used to be a famous maestro around here." Carter told him.

"But then something happened." Elodie explained, dramatically, "He stopped playing, and the theatre had to shut down. Remember we saw it in town, Jack? The orchestra quit because of the lack of wages. Mr Willows only teaches music now."

"Well, only to me." Carter muttered. "The only reason Mr Willows agreed is because my father is a good friend of his."

At that moment, Thomas stormed into the room, "Elodie? Jack? What are you doing here?" he demanded. "You don't have permission to be here!"

Elodie and Jack were speechless.

Carter spoke up, "I asked them to come, Mr Willows. Elodie and Jack were helping me practise."

Before Thomas could say anything else, Carter played "Nearer My God to Thee," the way Elodie and Jack explained it. With feeling. Thomas waited until the song was finished, and then cleared his throat,

"Carter, it seems as though you've learnt this song well. You are free to go if you'd like."

This took Carter by surprise. "Oh, um, thank you, sir." He hurriedly put his cello away and stood up. "See you next week."

Thomas nodded, "Until next week."

Elodie, Jack, and Carter silently walked down the corridor. Once they rounded the corner, Carter ran down the stairs and placed his cello to the side. He started to pull on his jacket.

"What's the rush?" Jack asked, hurrying after him.

"We're going outside, aren't we? We have exactly half an hour until my father comes to pick me up." Carter grinned. "Let's make the most of it."

5

Carter visited Jack and Elodie frequently during the next few weeks. They spent their time playing outside or talking in the library. Elodie and Carter still pretended to dislike each other, but Jack could tell they were becoming friends. Jack started to enjoy his time at the mansion. His days were filled with reading and spending time with Elodie and Carter. The only real problem was the church.

His aunt and uncle always left him behind on Sundays and went to church. They thought that it would be too hard for him to go. Thomas, however, would not hear of Jack staying behind. Everyone attended and Thomas said that he would not make an exception for Jack. At church, nobody bothered Jack. People stared at him and whispered as he walked by, but Thomas always left immediately after the service, and Jack joined him. Even though Elodie and Carter stayed.

One day, Jack, Elodie, and Carter were sitting in the library talking when Carter suddenly asked, "What do you usually do here at Christmas?"

"What made you think of Christmas?" Jack asked.

"It's in three days," Carter replied.

Jack was surprised. He had completely forgotten about Christmas.

"Mr Willows usually leaves early for work," Elodie said with a hint of sadness in her voice, "but he leaves us all presents under the tree."

"He goes to work on *Christmas*?" Carter asked.

Elodie nodded. Jack suddenly had an idea.

"Hey, why don't we leave Mr Willows a present before he leaves for work?" Jack suggested. "We could bake cookies and buy him a present."

"Yes!" Elodie cried, "And I could write a letter asking him to stay home this year!"

Carter snorted, "Just don't scare him, Elodie."

Elodie huffed, "You just see, Carter."

They spent the rest of the day planning what they would buy. The next day, Jack got a recipe from Marta and all of them pooled their money. Elodie went to town and bought a present. Then, she wrote Thomas a letter. Even Carter agreed that it was perfect.

* * *

Jack heard someone throwing stones at his window. He quickly got up and checked the time.

5:00.

According to Elodie, Thomas got up at 6:30 and left by 7:00. They had enough time to bake cookies. Jack went to his window and saw Carter waving. He hurried downstairs and let him in.

"Did you tell your parents?" Jack asked.

Carter nodded, "They know I'll spend the day here."

The boys went to the kitchen where Elodie already set up all the ingredients. She greeted them and they got to work.

"I don't see why we couldn't have just made the cookies yesterday," Carter said as he tried to beat eggs quietly.

"Because it'll be better if we leave Mr Willows *warm* cookies," Elodie replied.

Once they finished the cookies, Elodie set them on a plate and Jack got the envelope with the letter inside it and the present. They crept up to Thomas' room. All of them stood in front of his door and Carter pulled out three twigs.

"Seriously?" Elodie whispered.

"To see who goes in." Carter whispered back.

They all picked a twig. Elodie got the shortest.

"Curse you, Carter." she muttered.

Elodie tiptoed inside the room and placed the present and plate on Thomas' desk. She put the envelope on top of the present. Elodie was about to leave when something caught her eye under a stack of papers on the desk. She slowly slipped out a photograph from under them. She tried to look at it in the dark. Elodie could make out a woman with long dark hair, but who was that next to her?

Thomas stirred and Elodie dropped the photograph. She quickly picked it up and returned it to the desk. Then, she left the room.

"What took you so long?" Jack asked as they walked to his room.

"I saw a photo of a woman on Mr Willows' desk." Elodie said. "Isn't that strange?"

"Maybe he has a sweetheart." Carter suggested.

"I doubt it." Jack replied, "See you in the morning, Elodie."

"It *is* the morning." Elodie reminded him.

"Right." Jack grinned. "Merry Christmas."

* * *

The alarm clock on Thomas' dresser rang. He woke up and sat in bed for a while. He then got up and started to get ready. As he was dressing, Thomas spotted a plate and a small box on his desk. He went over to it. An envelope was placed on top of the box. Thomas opened it.

Dear Mr Willows, Uncle Thomas, Maestro, teacher,

As you can see, you have a lot of titles, just as you have a lot of work, and just as you have a lot of friends.

Every year at Christmas, you spend time with your work. So perhaps this year, you could spend it with your friends who are waiting downstairs?

It's certainly not as important as your job, but it's much more fun.
Yours Truly

Thomas was stunned. He had always thought that everyone *wanted* him to go to work on Christmas. He carefully unwrapped the present. Inside was a brand-new silver pocket watch.

Thomas picked up his telephone and started dialing.

A little while later, Elodie, Jack, and Carter rushed downstairs and into the main hall where the Christmas tree was set up. Everyone else was already there sitting around the tree talking. All three of them stopped short when they saw what was under the tree.

Absolutely nothing.

"Maybe he forgot." Theo suggested.

"I don't think he forgot." Elodie said quietly.

"Well, there's more to Christmas than presents." Marta said.

"I don't care about the presents, Marta." Jack said, "I'm just afraid we did something to hurt him."

Elodie and Carter nodded. At that moment, everyone heard someone coming down the stairs. A few seconds later, Thomas came into the room, his arms full of gifts.

"Good morning," Thomas said, smiling, "and Merry Christmas."

"Mr Willows!" Elodie exclaimed and ran over to help him.

Thomas sat down, "Sorry, I'm late, I had to call the lab and tell them I wasn't coming to work today."

Elodie, Jack, and Carter smiled at each other. Thomas started handing out gifts. Everyone couldn't suppress shouts of joy. Every year they usually got presents similar to the ones from the previous year. But this year, Thomas had actually spent time on their gifts.

Rogers and Theo had party suits with matching pants. Marta and Ansley had beautiful gowns. Elodie found a gold locket and earrings in her box. Even Carter had a present, which somewhat surprised him: a brand-new baseball and catching mitt.

But Jack thought he had the best present of them all. He carefully unwrapped the box and found a book inside: *The Call of the Wild* by Jack London.

Thomas leaned over and whispered, "Ansley told me you like to read. This isn't a new book, it's from my personal collection, but I think you'll like it."

The fact that Thomas had given him one of his own books made it all the more special to Jack. He smiled at him, "Thank you, Uncle Thomas."

Jack glanced over at Thomas one more time. He was smiling and looking at everyone admiring their presents.

His right hand was fidgeting with a silver pocket watch.

6

Thomas started to act nicer towards Jack. Their conversations were freer, and Thomas wasn't so distant, but he still remained unapproachable in a few aspects. Jack's time there became busy but enjoyable. At least until Thomas announced that he would be starting school in two days.

"School?" Jack asked, he touched his scar.

Thomas nodded, "I would get you a tutor, but it seems like a waste of money. The school is well-known for its academics. I attended it when I was your age. Elodie goes there as well, so you won't be alone."

Jack tried to smile. He always had tutors in the past. His uncle and aunt agreed that school would be somewhat difficult for him. But Jack didn't want to argue with Thomas, so he agreed.

Theo got him all the supplies he needed. Elodie spent the next day explaining to Jack everything they had learnt during the past few months. Jack woke up the next morning wishing he were dead.

* * *

Elodie and Jack walked to school together. Although Elodie tried to act confident, Jack could see that even she was worried. The school was just ten minutes away. It was a two-story, red-brick building, surrounded by white pebbles. The field was filled with children of all ages, laughing, talking, and playing. Elodie and Jack stood talking when Elodie waved to a girl behind Jack.

"I'll be right back." Elodie said and ran over to the girl.

The second Elodie stepped away, a boy who looked about fifteen, walked over to Jack. A few others followed.

"Hey, kid." he said, "I'm Harold Peters. You're new, right?"

Jack nodded.

"Well, maybe you can help me." Harold said, "I'm looking for a new kid named Jack. Have you seen him?"

Jack's heart pounded. Why was this boy looking for him?

"Jack? No, I haven't. M-my name's Carter."

Just then, Elodie ran over to Jack. She was calling his name. The other kids laughed and made a circle around Jack.

"Well, *Carter*," Harold sneered, "is Jack your middle name, or your spy name? Why are you here? To give information to the Japanese?"

This confused Jack. "What?"

Harold didn't answer. In one motion, he grabbed the end of Jack's scarf and yanked it off. Jack spun around twice and fell.

"Would you look at that," Harold shouted. "He's hideous, along with everything else!"

Along with everything else?

What was this boy talking about?

"Get lost, Harold!" Elodie shouted. She was suddenly at Jack's side, forming a densely packed snowball.

"*You* get lost, servant girl." Harold snarled. "This doesn't concern you."

Elodie took Jack's arm and tried to walk away, but Harold grabbed Jack's elbow and pulled them back. Faster than you could blink, Elodie shoved the hard, frozen snowball in Harold's mouth. Everyone went silent. Harold spat out a bloody snowball, along with a tooth. Elodie walked away smiling and pulling Jack behind her. No one tried to stop them.

"You haven't heard the last of this, Elodie!" Harold roared. "I will have vengeance!"

* * *

The rest of the week was highly confusing to Jack. All the students avoided him, which wasn't peculiar because of his scar. But something told him that his scar wasn't the only reason. Even his teachers acted strangely around him. Always whispering to one another when his back was turned.

Jack asked Elodie if she knew anything about what was happening, but she didn't. The week finally ended, and Jack looked forward to the weekend. Carter came over the next day, and Jack complained to him.

"It's the weirdest thing." Jack said. "It's one thing to be bullied about this stupid scar, but people are calling me 'spy' and 'traitor'. They don't even know me!"

Carter was about to say something when Thomas hurried into the room.

"What did they call you?" he demanded.

"Pardon?" asked Jack.

"*What did they call you?*" Thomas repeated.

"Um, 'traitor' and 'spy'."

"But did they say anything else, Jack?" Thomas asked, shaking him by the shoulders.

"No. Uncle Thomas."

Thomas straightened himself out and cleared his throat, "Jack, it seems school isn't working for you. I shall hire a tutor for you. You will start this Monday."

Jack nodded.

"Can I be tutored as well?" Elodie asked.

"No." Thomas answered and left.

"That was weird," Carter said.

"And rude." Elodie added.

"He looked afraid, didn't he?" Carter said.

Jack shrugged, "At least I don't have to go to school anymore."

Jack's tutor was named Steven Montgomery. He was a good teacher and made Jack work hard. Best of all, he never complained about how Jack looked.

As the days grew warmer Jack, Elodie, and Carter spent most of their time outside. They visited Tyler and Marie often and gave performances at the music store. Although Jack never participated, no matter how much Elodie and Carter begged.

Spring was especially rainy that year. After the rainy season started, Jack, Elodie, and Carter could only stay inside. Marta wouldn't let them play outside.

"Don't you children go on getting sick, now." she had said, "I'll be the one looking after you if you do."

Carter had invited them over to his house one day, but that hadn't gone over well. Particularly because Elodie had tormented

Carter's mother's cat by putting her outside in the rain. In Mr Willows Mansion, they explored every room they were allowed to go into. The only room left unexplored was the Music Room. The three of them sat in the living room silently.

"I'm bored." Elodie complained.

"Let's go visit Tyler and Marie." Jack suggested.

"They're closed on Sundays, remember?" Carter told him.

"Right." Jack said. Then, his face brightened, "Let's ask Uncle Thomas if we can go into the Music Room."

Carter looked at him as though he'd lost his mind, "Are you nuts? We'd be lucky to come back with our lives."

Jack rolled his eyes, "He isn't as bad as all that. Come on."

They followed Jack to the library. The door was closed.

"You should go in, Elodie." Jack said.

"Me?" Elodie cried quietly.

Carter nodded, "He's more likely to listen to a girl."

Elodie raised her eyebrows, "Oh yeah? How come you never listen to me?"

"Because I'm not an idiot." Carter said, "Now, go on."

Elodie took a deep breath and walked inside, leaving the door open a smidge.

Thomas looked up from his book, "Hello, Elodie."

"Hi, Mr Willows." Elodie greeted. "W-we, I mean, I was just wondering if- you see I..." She bit her nail nervously.

"Pull yourself together, child. I'm not going to murder you." Thomas said. "What is it?"

Elodie looked around helplessly, "I just wanted permission to use the Music Room because it's kind of dumb to let it sit there rotting while we could be practising, and-" Elodie clamped her mouth shut before she could say anything else.

Thomas actually started laughing. Outside the library, Carter and Jack looked at each other in amazement.

"He's either in shock or maniacal murder mood." said Carter.

"Shut up." whispered Jack.

"Come here," Thomas told Elodie.

Elodie cautiously stepped forward.

"Rest in peace, Elodie." Carter whispered outside.

Jack shushed him.

Thomas took Elodie's hand in his, "You amuse me, Elodie. You, Jack, and Carter may use the Music Room whenever you'd like."

Elodie was taken aback for a second, "Thanks, Mr Willows!" she cried.

Elodie ran out of the room and past Carter and Jack to the Music Room. The boys followed her. Once they got there, Elodie sat on the piano bench and opened the lid. They played song after song, improvising them and having fun. Jack sat and watched.

"I know!" Elodie exclaimed suddenly, "Mr Willows' birthday is in two weeks. All of us should play something for him."

Carter agreed, but Jack shook his head.

"I don't play." he said.

"Honestly, Jack." Elodie said impatiently. "Would you tell us why?"

Jack remained silent.

"Jack," Elodie persisted.

"Leave him be, Elodie." Carter said.

"Well, it's just silly not to play when you can. If we're real friends you should at least tell us *why*."

Jack bit his lip. He had to tell them now, or else it would seem like he didn't trust his friends.

Jack sighed, "I don't play music anymore because I'm cursed."

7

Elodie and Carter stared at him.

"You don't play music because you're cursed?" Elodie repeated, unable to stop herself from laughing.

"I'm serious, Elodie." Jack said looking down.

"Explain." Carter said.

"I don't know exactly what happened, but this is what my uncle told me," Jack started. "When I was a baby-maybe eight months, or so-I found my father's violin and started playing with it. Apparently, my father was supposed to be watching me, but he got distracted. I started twisting the pegs. I went too far with one of them, and a string snapped and slashed me across the face.

"The doctor was new and couldn't stitch me up well. I've looked like *this* ever since." Jack gestured angrily to his face, "My parents made me take violin lessons, but my teacher said nobody would ever want to hear me play because I look so scary. I just stopped trying after a while."

"Oh, Jack," Elodie said gently, "that scar doesn't mean you're cursed. That violin teacher was wrong. *Please* play something with us, and you'll see that you're perfectly normal."

Jack was quiet for a second. He looked at Carter and Elodie's eager faces, "Ok, I'll try something."

Elodie clapped her hands and ran over to a shelf. She pulled out a music book and opened it to "Nearer My God to Thee". Jack carefully got a violin cast and opened it. He made sure the instrument was in tune. He looked over the music and tried the first few notes. Jack's hands shook. He nodded to Elodie, and she began with the opening piano chords. Carter joined in.

Jack took a deep breath and began to play. The most beautiful sound wafted through the room. The majestic sound of the cello, the harmonious piano. Both mixed with the sweet violin. Jack closed his eyes and played, and nothing else mattered. The last notes came, and they all ended with a flourish.

Jack grinned, "That sounded amazing."

"We've got to play something for Mr Willows' birthday." Elodie said. "He'll love it."

She and Carter looked at Jack.

"Let's do it." said Jack.

* * *

That day, all of them looked for the right piece to play. Although they found many pieces that sounded nice, none of them seemed perfect. Jack was looking through the shelves in the music room and found something out of place: a leather-bound book.

"Hey, what's this?" Jack asked.

Carter and Elodie went over to him.

"Looks like a diary." said Carter.

Jack opened it, and a sheet of paper fell out. He picked it up and examined it. It was a score sheet for "O My Love Is Like A Red Red Rose".

"Why don't we play this?" Jack said looking at it, "It's a good song."

Elodie and Carter agreed.

"We probably shouldn't read the diary." Carter said, seeing Elodie's prying eyes.

Jack nodded and closed the book. He put it back on the shelf. He caught a glimpse of a name inside the diary before he closed it.

Jane.

Jack put the name into his memory.

8

Springville, Utah
1899

Akari put down her suitcase and looked around the empty house. Her husband, Yohei, came up behind her a few seconds later.

"What do you think?" he asked in Japanese.

"This house is much bigger than our old one, Yohei." Akari replied. "Do you think we'll be able to fit in in this country?"

"Of course, we will."

"We don't even know English."

"We will learn." Yohei replied in English.

Akari laughed at his accent.

"Our future lies here, Akari." Yohei said and placed a kiss on her cheek.

Akari and Yohei were a Japanese couple that immigrated to America. Yohei had received a job working for the railroad in Utah, and they moved immediately. Although Akari had doubts about moving, she happily settled into her new home. Five years later, Akari and Yohei were leading happy lives in America. They had worked hard to integrate into the culture. They soon found out that they were going to have a child. They had a beautiful baby girl with big dark eyes and a lovely smile.

They didn't name her until she was three months old. Only then did they find the right name.

Jane

It was perfect.

* * *

Jane fit in well in America. She spoke English fluently, and the only indication that she was Japanese was her face. Jane attended the Springville Public School and made many friends. Everyone was fascinated with Jane and would always ask her to speak Japanese. Although Jane loved her life in America, she longed to know more about her ancestral home. So, after she finished college, Jane went to Japan in search of a job. Jane's parents, who were content with their lives, let Jane go, but with the promise that she would return.

And so, Jane's new life began.

Jane made many friends in Japan and learnt more about her culture. She stayed with some of her relatives who were amazed at Jane's skill in music, physical activities, and academics. Jane didn't have to search for a job, rather the job found her.

This job in Japan was only for the brilliant. Those who had the sharpest minds and the cunning of a fox. It required Jane to stay focused and to be present at any time needed.

And to keep a diary.

9

Springville, Utah
April 1954

It was Thomas' birthday. Carter and Elodie sat nervously in the Music Room with the rest of the staff. Jack was downstairs convincing Thomas to go up.

"Should we practice?" Elodie asked.

Carter shook his head, "My dad said if you practise right before a performance, you'll burst a blood vessel or something." He bit his lip, "Do you think he'll like it?"

Both Marta and Rogers nodded.

"He'll love it." said Marta.

"I, for one, can't wait to hear what you've prepared." Theo said.

A few seconds later, Jack and Thomas walked into the room. Everyone stood up.

"Happy Birthday!" they all chorused.

Thomas smiled. "Thank you. What is this all about?"

Rogers pulled a chair for Thomas, "The children have prepared something for you."

Elodie, Jack, and Carter readied their instruments. Then, Elodie played the opening notes, and the sweet sound of "O My Love" filled the room. Everyone was mesmerised by the music.

Only Ansley noticed that something was wrong.

While everyone sat stock-still, looking at the children, Thomas abruptly looked away. He clenched his fists, and Ansley saw his eyes fill with tears. Thomas suddenly stood in the middle of the song and stormed out of the room. Everyone was momentarily shocked. Then, Ansley ran after Thomas. She found him in the entrance hall putting on his hat.

"Mr Willows?"

"Ansley, I'm going out." Thomas said. "Tell Jack, Elodie, and Carter they're not allowed to use the Music Room anymore."

"But, Mr Willows, they were only-"

"Just do it!" Thomas yelled.

Ansley shrunk back, "Yes, sir." she whispered.

Back in the Music Room, Jack, Elodie, and Carter sat silently.

"What did we do now?" Elodie asked.

Marta sighed, "I don't know, Elodie."

"It's my fault, isn't it?" Jack spoke up suddenly.

"What?" Carter asked.

"He left because I played," Jack shook his head. "I told you I'm cursed."

* * *

That day was miserable. Everyone dawdled around, not knowing what to do. Ansley told Jack, Carter, and Elodie that they weren't allowed in the Music Room anymore. Carter and Elodie were sad, but Jack didn't care. Or at least he pretended not to. In truth, the only reason Jack wanted to go back to the Music Room was to get a hold of that diary.

Jack suspected it would have some answers as to why Thomas acted so strange. But since the Music Room was banned, Jack could not investigate.

Not during the day, anyways.

That evening, Jack ate quickly and excused himself to his room. He paced in his room impatiently and waited for everyone to go to bed. Thomas returned at around eleven and went straight to his room, refusing Marta's offers of food. Jack stood at his bedroom door and took a deep breath. He peeked outside into the dark corridor and tiptoed outside.

He walked a bit faster once he got to the third floor. Jack slowly opened the door to the Music Room and went to the glass cupboard. He found the diary and made his way back.

Mission accomplished. Jack thought as he reached his bedroom. Then he heard something. Jack stopped walking to listen better. It was coming from the second last door in the corridor.

Thomas' bedroom.

Jack's mind told himself to go back to his room, but curiosity got the better of him. He silently walked to Thomas' room and gave the door a small push. Thomas was sitting on his bed; his back was turned to the door. He was in a hunched position, as though he was crying. After a few moments, Jack realised that he *was* crying.

Jack watched for a moment, deciding whether he should talk to him or just leave. Thomas got up to close the window, and Jack quickly stepped back. Before Jack left, he saw Thomas wiping his tears and looking at a photograph he clutched in his hand.

Jack thought about what he saw once he got back to his room. He sat on his bed thinking. Why was Thomas crying? It surely had to be something bigger than a song. He looked at the diary in his hand. Maybe this would have some answers.

Jack was about to open it, but then he started to feel guilty. This wasn't any of his business. But he had to know why today's events happened. Was it because of his curse, or something else?

Jack opened the diary. The page directly after the cover had the name, *Jane Sasaki*, written on it. Folded inside the book was a withered rose. Jack carefully brushed the rose, and a petal fell out from his touch. Jack opened to the next page and suppressed an angry yell. He wanted to kick something.

Everything was in Japanese.

10

Springville, Utah
1930

Two years later, Jane returned to America, but her job in Japan remained. At the moment, she didn't have to do much work, but her company promised her the time would come when they would need Jane.

At the news of her return to America, all of Jane's friends threw a big celebration for her. Her parents were overjoyed to see her again, and everyone was very curious about her job. Although Jane could tell her friends and family very little, she happily explained all that she could.

Jane was surprised to see how much her friends had changed during the time she was gone. Her two closest friends, Anna and Richard, had gotten married.

"Congratulations!" Jane cried when she found out, "I always knew you two were for each other."

Anna smiled, "We wanted to hold the wedding after you returned, but we couldn't wait."

Jane assured her that it was no problem.

"Jane!" a voice cried out.

Jane's friend Thomas ran over to her and hugged her.

"You're finally back!" Thomas said. "The orchestra is completely lost without you."

Richard nodded, "We can't play a single right note."

Jane laughed, "I can't wait to start playing again. I've missed you all so much."

The four friends spent a long time talking. They helped clean up after the party was over and talked about old times.

"Oh, I got all of you presents." Jane said. She went to her room and got the gifts out of her bag.

She went back down and handed each of them a brown-leather journal.

"I have one just like it." Jane said. "Do you remember how we all wanted matching things when we were young?"

Everyone laughed.

"Well, it's getting late. We better get going." Richard said standing.

"Thanks for the party." Jane said.

Jane walked with her friends to the gate. After Richard and Anna left, Thomas turned to Jane. He handed her, rather bashfully, a rose quickly walked away. Jane smiled with surprise and smelled the rose. She realised that she was still holding her leather journal.

Jane carefully pressed the rose between its pages.

11

Springville, Utah
June 1954

During the last few months of school, Jack hardly saw Thomas. He left early for work and returned home late. He gave Carter's parents excuses every week to skip Carter's music lessons. Thomas isolated himself and took his meals in his room. Whatever Jack, Elodie, and Carter had done had wounded him badly.

Jack occupied himself with studying and reading. He was convinced, now more than ever, that he was cursed. He thought that his scar was a sign that whenever he played music, it would only bring sadness, even though Elodie told him that there were no such things as curses.

Unlike Thomas, Jack did not isolate himself. He spent more time with Carter and Elodie, trying to figure out what went wrong. It hardly rained anymore, and they spent every second outside.

"I can't wait until school is over." Elodie said, sitting on the branch of a tree in the backyard.

"I *wish* I could go to school," Carter said wistfully. "but mother says, 'tutors are much more educational'." he imitated her voice.

Elodie giggled.

"What 'bout you, Jack?" Carter asked.

Jack was sitting on the grass and looking at the mansion.

"Jack?" Carter repeated.

"What?" Jack asked.

Elodie sighed, "You're no fun anymore, Jack. All you do is think."

Jack glared at her, "Well, I've been thinking of important things. For example, what did we do to make Uncle Thomas give us the silent treatment?"

"I have no idea." Carter said.

Jack stood up and rubbed his head, "I saw him crying that night when he got back home. Why-"

"He was *crying*?" Elodie cried.

Jack nodded. Everyone thought for a while.

"We have to ask someone," Elodie said. "but who?"

"None of the staff." Carter said, "They don't seem to know anything either."

"What about Tyler and Marie?" Jack suggested.

"How could they help?" Elodie asked. "They hardly know Mr Willows."

Jack shrugged, "It's worth a shot."

They went to the front gate and started walking. Jack kept his face down and avoided people's eyes. He looked at Carter walking with his head up. Jack sighed, what he wouldn't give to be a normal boy. They hurried to the music store and went inside. Marie greeted them as they entered.

"We haven't seen you in a while." she said. "Here for another performance? No one else will hear it, unfortunately." she gestured to the empty store.

"Thanks, Marie," Carter said, "but we're not here to play instruments. We have some questions."

Marie smiled, "We were just about to have tea. Why don't all of you join us?"

She led them to the back of the store where her kitchen was. Tyler was sitting at a small round table sipping tea. He greeted everyone when they walked in. They all sat down, and after a few pleasantries, Jack got to the reason they came.

He told Tyler and Marie what happened on Thomas' birthday and what he saw that night. After he finished talking, Maria and Tyler glanced at each other nervously.

Marie put her teacup down, "A long time ago, we made a promise to keep a secret. The questions you ask might reveal the secret, so we cannot answer everything."

Jack, Elodie, and Carter looked down with disappointment.

"But we *can* tell you something." Tyler said reassuringly. "I'll tell you a story. Once upon a time, Thomas Willows was the most famous maestro in Springville. He had a huge orchestra and there were queues that wound down the streets. His performances were magical. Sometimes, Mr Willows would write plays for his music. But one day, something happened. Mr Willows shut himself away, ashamed, and afraid of the mistakes he made. His orchestra was lost without him and had to permanently close. I think the particular song you played on his birthday reminded him of his greatest mistake."

"But why did he take it out on us?" Elodie asked.

"Because he had no one else to be angry at." Marie explained. "But I assure all of you, you were not the reason Thomas was crying."

"Jack saw Mr Willows holding a photograph while he was crying," Carter said. "Do you have any idea what that might be about?"

Tyler sighed, "I'm afraid we can't tell you that, Carter."

"How do you know so much about Uncle Thomas anyway?" Jack asked.

Tyler and Marie looked at each other again.

"Do you promise to never tell anyone?" Marie asked, looking at each of them.

They all nodded.

"We know him because...because our last name is also Willows," Tyler told them.

Carter and Jack's mouths fell open, and Elodie said a very unpleasant word.

"You mean you and Tyler are..." Jack gasped.

"Yes, Jack," Tyler said, sighing, "we are Thomas' parents."

12

Jack, Elodie, and Carter walked back home in a daze. Jack was so surprised he forgot to hide his scar. Carter finally swallowed and said something.

"Mr Willows is their *son*? Why doesn't anyone know, then?"

Jack and Elodie shrugged. They were too stunned to speak. The whole weekend, they tried to figure out why Thomas wouldn't want anyone to know that Tyler and Marie were his parents. All their guesses seemed wrong or far-fetched. Jack became worried, though. What were Thomas' mistakes? Did Thomas cast his parents out because they were going to spill his secrets?

It was scary seeing Thomas go to bed every night. Jack held his breath until he passed by.

It was the last day of school, at least for Elodie. Carter and Jack's tutoring ended one week early. Elodie was furious, but Ansley made her go to school anyway. Everyone was acting strange. They kept asking Elodie about Jack. She only said that he was fine and ignored all their questions and comments. Her friend Catherine tried to get her to tell her more but failed.

"Did you hear the rumour?" Catherine asked as they were walking home.

"About whom?" Elodie questioned.

"That boy who's living at your place."

Elodie glared at Catherine, "His name is Jack, and he's my friend. I don't want to hear anything about him."

"But Elodie, you have to be careful of him!" Catherine cried, "He's-"

"Stop it, Cat!" Elodie said and walked in front of her. Elodie ignored her until she arrived home. Catherine apologised and wished her a nice summer.

Elodie walked through the front yard and thought about what Catherine had said. *You have to be careful of him.* Why would she have to be careful of Jack? He was just a boy. Elodie pushed the thoughts away and walked into the kitchen where Jack and Carter were eating cookies.

Elodie threw her school bag on the ground and joined them.

"Finally," she said, "two months of no studying."

"Good luck with that, Elodie." Marta said, kneading dough. "Ansley will make you read every day."

Elodie shrugged, "Two months of no Harold Peters then."

"What's Harold's problem with me anyway?" Jack asked. "His father owns Peters' Bakery, right? He also seemed weird when I first met him."

"Don't you worry about that, Jack," Marta said. "It's summer, and you should be outside. Stop eating all my cookies."

Marta shooed them all outside. They went to the backyard and started climbing trees. Carter settled himself on a branch and looked at the forest behind the house.

"Why do you think we're not allowed to go in there?" he asked.

"There's probably a gold mine in there, and Mr Willows doesn't want us to discover it." Elodie said.

Jack and Carter smiled.

"Let's go in." Elodie said.

Jack shook his head, "It's a forbidden area, Elodie."

"Come on." Elodie said, jumping off the tree. "Don't be so boring."

She ran into the forest.

Carter and Jack looked at each other.

"We're not going to let her die in there, are we?" Jack asked.

"Tempting, but no." Carter said. He ran after Elodie, with Jack following.

They found Elodie looking at something on the ground. The forest was thick with trees. Sunlight shone through the leaves, illuminating the forest. The occasional squirrel jumped from a tree and scurried back up.

"What is that?" Elodie asked.

She pointed to a stone slab, curved at the top, and covered by moss. In front of it was a box made of white stone.

"It looks like a gravestone." Jack said, "Wh- why would there be a gravestone in Uncle Thomas' forest?"

"Let's see whose name is on it." Elodie said, bending down to wipe the moss off.

"Wait," Carter said, "this feels wrong. We should either uncover the stone or open the box."

They all looked at each other.

"The box." they said in unision.

Carter carefully picked it up and started to scratch of the moss that covered it. He looked at Elodie and Jack and nervously slid off the heavy lid.

"How curious." he said when he saw the contents.

Inside was a hard piece of paper turned upside down and a leather journal. Jack, Elodie, and Carter sat down to inspect everything. First, Carter opened the journal. It was empty, except for the name *Thomas Willows* on the first page. Then he picked up the piece of paper and turned it right side up. Everyone gasped when they saw what was written on it.

Marriage Certificate

This is to Certify that

Thomas Willows *And* Jane Sasaki

Were Wed on the 23 Day of June In the Year 1936 .

By: Rev. James White

At: Springville Church, Utah .

Bride

Groom

Elodie made a sound which sounded like a cross between a scream and a gasp. Carter started breathing heavily, and Jack just stared at the certificate. Then Elodie investigated the box and saw a photograph of a woman. She gasped.

"This is the photo I saw on Christmas," Elodie said, "and maybe the one Mr Willows was holding when he was crying. This woman looks Asian."

Jack looked at the photograph and then at the gravestone. He couldn't take it anymore. He stood up and quickly started to scrape the moss off the stone. He stood up and looked at it when he was done. Jack rubbed his temples as though he could wipe away his headache. Carter and Elodie stood beside him.

The gravestone said:

In loving memory of
Jane Sasaki Willows
Beloved Daughter and Wife
April 26, 1904-November 8, 1943

Jack, Elodie, and Carter stood in absolute shock. Finally, Elodie swallowed and cried hoarsely,

"Mr Willows was *married*?"

13

Springville, Utah
1936

Jane laughed as Anna and Marie fastened her veil. Her mother, Akari, made the finishing touches on her velvet dress. Lace was tied around her waist, and a pearl border was on the top of her dress. The skirt came down in multiple layers so that it looked like a cloud. Marie fixed her hair and stepped back to look at her.

Marie drew in a breath, "Jane, my girl, you look beautiful."

Anna nodded, "An actual princess."

Akari smiled at her, and Anna took Jane's hands in hers.

"I'm so nervous, Anna." Jane said, but she was smiling.

"Honestly, me too," Anna said, "but so excited!"

Jane and Anna laughed like schoolgirls.

Richard stuck his head from behind the door, "Wow." he said, smiling. "Come on, it's starting."

Anna and Jane walked out of the room. Yohei was waiting outside. Anna wished Jane luck and went inside the church with Richard. Jane took her father's arm and smiled at him. The doors to the church opened, and everyone inside stood up. Yohei and Jane walked down the aisle. Thomas was waiting at the front of the church. He looked equally as nervous as Jane, but his eyes projected love and adoration.

The service was joyous. The reception afterwards was very chaotic with everyone congratulating Thomas and Jane. People showered them with gifts. It lasted well into the evening. Anna and Richard did not leave Jane and Thomas' side until the end.

"I guess you're Mrs Willows, now." said Richard laughing.

Jane smiled, "I will never get tired of hearing that."

* * *

Thomas and Jane were a very happy couple. Thomas was a maestro, and Jane played as a violinist in his orchestra. They gave performances together, and they were both loving and friendly. They loved each other very much and hardly ever fought. Thomas and Jane, Jane and Thomas. That's how it was.

If only they knew they would soon be torn apart.

14

Springville, Utah
June 1954

Jack, Elodie, and Carter sat on the forest floor in stunned silence. Why was Thomas' wife's grave in the forest? Why did no one know about this?

"What do we do now?" Elodie asked, biting her nail.

Jack took a deep breath, "We keep this a secret between us." he said. "Uncle Thomas obviously hasn't seen the grave in a while. Look at the moss covering it. We won't tell anyone about what we found. Promise?"

Carter and Elodie nodded, "Promise."

All of them got up. Jack picked up the heavy box, and they quietly left the forest.

"We have to find out more about this," Carter said. "But where can we look? We can't ask anyone, or they'll ask how we know about Mr Willows' wife."

"I know!" Elodie exclaimed.

"Shh." Jack said.

"We look in the attic," Elodie said, more quietly. "I've only been there once, but there are so many boxes and stuff up there. We're bound to find something."

Carter and Jack agreed.

"We have to do it now." Elodie said. "Mr Willows is still at work."

All of them walked back to the house. Jack hurried to his room and put the box under his bed. Then, they ran up to the third floor.

"I didn't know this place had an attic." Carter said.

"We didn't know this place had hidden gravestones either." Jack said.

Carter shrugged, "Fair enough."

Elodie got a chair from the Music Room and dragged it to the centre of the corridor. She climbed onto it and pressed a wood panel on the ceiling. The panel opened and Elodie pulled out a loft ladder. She climbed up, and Carter and Jack followed. The attic was a dusty place with a small, round window on one side. It was filled with boxes and old, broken things.

"I guess we search now," Elodie said. "Look for anything with the name *Jane*."

They began looking through boxes. Most of them were filled with ripped-up books and old toys. As Elodie looked around, she saw an old violin case with the name *Richard* on it. She was about to go to it when Carter said, "The gravestone said that Jane died in 1943. She died during World War II."

"And?" Elodie asked, "A lot of people died during the war."

"Well, do you remember when all the Japanese people were taken into internment camps during that time? The photograph of Jane looked like she was Japanese," Carter said.

"Good point, Carter," Jack said, "maybe her death had something to do with World War II."

"But why would Mr Willows hide her grave in a forest?" Carter swallowed. "Do you think he, um, killed her?"

Elodie rolled her eyes, "Don't be an idiot, Carter. Mr Willows wouldn't kill his own wife."

They continued to search but found nothing. Then, Jack came across a small box filled with envelopes. He opened one and read it.

"I found something!" he cried.

Carter and Elodie went to him. He read the letter out loud.

"'Dear Thomas, I have recently finished my second year of university. I received a job in a small organisation. The work is hard, but I enjoy it. How are you doing? I hope your doctorate is going well. I, myself, haven't the courage to pursue it! Yours truly, Jane'."

"The stamp is from Japan," said Elodie.

She dug in the box full of envelopes and found a more recent date. There was no stamp on it, just the name *Thomas* and the date. She opened it and read out loud.

"'My dearest Thomas, It is my hope that you never have to read this letter, but if you do, I suppose you know everything now. Something has probably happened to me. Please forgive me for not telling you; I took an oath that I would tell no one. Please do not blame yourself if I die. I assure you it was not your fault. We are all destined to die. Life is only special because it ends. Live your life to the fullest. Love, Jane."'

"Wow." said Carter once Elodie finished, "What do you think she did?"

"I don't know, but it must've been bad if she had to die for it." Jack said. "There has to be some explanation here."

They kept on reading letters.

* * *

Thomas walked back from work deep in thought. He had much to do in the week. As he looked around, he saw a woman with long dark hair and dark eyes. He blinked.

"Jane?" he whispered.

Thomas blinked again and he saw a stranger. Thomas breathed heavily, he clutched the rail and tried to steady his breath.

"Are you alright, sir?" asked a young girl looking at him.

Thomas tried to smile, "I'm fine, thank you."

He steadied himself and walked home. Rogers met him at the door and took his hat.

Upstairs in the attic, Jack, Elodie, and Carter heard the door slam. They looked at each other.

"He's back!" Elodie cried. "Hurry!"

They put the letters back in the box and scrambled down the ladder. Elodie closed the panel and lugged the chair back to the Music Room. Just in time. Thomas walked up the steps and looked at them.

"What are you three up to?" he asked.

"Um, nothing, Mr Willows," Elodie said.

She grabbed Jack and Carter by the elbows and dragged them to the kitchen. They sat at the table gasping.

"That was close," Jack said, "too close."

"And we haven't found out much." Carter said.

Elodie bit her lip, "There is *one* place we haven't looked."

"Where?" Jack asked.

"Mr Willows' Study."

"Are you insane?" Carter asked. "He'll murder us if he catches us in there."

"So we'll go when he's at work." Elodie said. "We have a good chance of finding something in there."

"I don't think that's a good idea." Carter said.

They both looked at Jack.

Jack nodded, "We have to do it." he said. "We're much too deep into this to stop now."

15

The next day, Thomas left for work in the morning. Carter arrived an hour later. Marta would not hear of Jack, Elodie, and Carter doing anything without eating. So, they ate a very big breakfast and went to find Theo. He was in the backyard tending to the garden. He greeted them when they walked up to him.

"Theo, we need a favour." Jack said, seriously.

"What kind of favour?" Theo asked, matching Jack's seriousness.

Elodie hesitated, "We-we are going on a dangerous quest."

"To find the truth." Carter joined in.

"For justice and honour." Jack said.

A smile tugged on the corner of Theo's mouth. "And what do you need from me?"

"If Mr Willows comes home, distract him as long as you can." Elodie said.

Theo gave them a skeptical look, "As long as you don't kill yourselves. Ok, I'll-"

"Thanks, Theo." Jack said, and they all ran off.

They made sure no one was looking and went to the second floor. Elodie looked around one more time and opened the door to Thomas' Study.

"Carter, stay by the door and be on the lookout for Mr Willows." Elodie said. "Jack and I will look around."

They searched for a long time. Jack and Elodie looked through books and drawers but found nothing. They were about to give up. Then, Elodie saw a small drawer on Thomas' desk. She carefully opened it and found a crumpled piece of paper inside. She smoothed it out and read it out loud.

"Listen to this," she said, "'Dear Jane, My days are filled with grief for you. I realise my horrible mistake now that you are gone. I know it will be very hard for you, but please forgive me. My pride blinded me from seeing how much I love you. I will make...' It ends there." Elodie said.

"It must be written by Mr Willows." Carter whispered. "I wonder what he did that was so awful."

As Jack looked over it, Carter heard footsteps.

"Someone is coming!" he exclaimed, "Hide!"

Jack and Carter quickly hid behind the curtains and Elodie somehow fit into a cupboard. Someone entered the room. Jack peeked through the curtains. It was Thomas. Jack's heart raced. Thomas would see the letter and the open drawer. Thomas went to his desk and sat. How were they going to get out?

Then, there was a knock on the door. Thomas gave his permission to enter, and Theo came in.

"Um, Mr Willows, I just planted two types of flowers and I was wondering which you would prefer." Theo said.

"Anything is fine, Theo." Thomas replied.

"Perhaps you should come to see them." Theo said. "I'd hate to plant something that ruins that beautiful garden."

Thomas sighed but followed Theo to the garden.

Good old Theo! Jack thought and came out from his hiding place.

Elodie fell from the cupboard and rubbed her back.

"Let's go." Carter said.

They ran out of the study and into Jack's bedroom. All of them fell to the ground once they got there.

"We owe Theo one." Elodie said. "I still have the letter."

Jack shot up, "What? He'll realise it's missing! Stay here."

Jack ran back to the Study and shoved the letter back into the drawer. He ran back out. Right into Thomas.

Thomas caught Jack by the shoulders, "Jack? What were you doing in there?" he demanded.

Jack was speechless.

"Answer me, you useless boy!" Thomas roared. "Why were you in my Study without permission? Really, you're just like your father."

Jack stopped struggling. He never properly knew his father. Jack didn't know the type of man he was, but he felt a sudden urge to defend him.

"You never even knew my father!" Jack cried. "You can't just say things like that!"

"You will not speak to me like that in my own house!" Thomas said.

Suddenly Elodie and Carter were by his side.

"Don't shout at him, Mr Willows!" she cried, "It was my idea! Jack had nothing to do with it!"

"All of you listen to me," Thomas said angrily, "I have been very generous to you. You run around in my house and are deafeningly loud. The least you can do is respect my privacy. I do not want to see any of you here ever again. Understand?"

Elodie and Carter nodded. They led Jack back to his room. Jack sniffled and wiped his eyes.

"I don't care anymore." Jack said. "I don't care about Uncle Thomas, or Jane, or what happened to them."

"That's alright, Jack." Carter said. "I don't want to investigate anymore either."

"Neither do I." Elodie said, "Let's just have as much fun as we can while you're still here."

Elodie's words struck pain into Jack's heart. He had forgotten that he would have to leave soon.

16

Springville, Utah
December 1941

The bell rang as Jane walked into Anna's Place.

Anna greeted her, "What do you think?" she asked, gesturing to the new music store she and Richard had opened.

"It's beautiful, Anna." Jane said.

Anna noticed that Jane looked a bit nervous. She invited her to tea, and they talked for a while.

"Did you hear about the bombing at Pearl Harbour?" Anna asked.

"Who hasn't?" Jane replied, "No one will even look at me anymore."

Anna patted her hand, "Are your parents alright?"

"For now." Jane said. She bit her lip.

"What's wrong, Jane?" Anna asked.

"Japanese citizens are being put in internment camps, Anna." Jane said. "I'm just afraid."

Anna talked to her for a while, assuring her that everything would be alright. Then she realised that Jane was holding a violin case.

Jane handed the case to Anna.

"Do you think you can take care of this for me?" she asked, "If they take me away, I want my violin to stay safe."

"Don't worry, Jane. I'll protect it with my life." Anna said. "I promise."

17

Springville, Utah
June 1954

Carter kicked a pebble on the street as the three of them walked to The Peters Bakery for Thomas' strawberry tarts. Jack, Elodie, and Carter had spent the last few days spending time together. They tried to have fun, but the reminder that Jack would have to leave in a week seemed to weigh on them.

They arrived at the bakery and got the tarts. As they were walking home, Elodie had a strange feeling that they were being followed. She turned and saw Harold and a few others quietly following them.

Once she saw them, Harold ran in front of them and blocked their path.

"Long time no see, traitor." Harold said. "So what have you been up to?"

Jack sighed in irritation, "Can you just let us go, please? I'm really not in the mood."

"No, I can't just let you go," Harold replied. "I'm conducting an investigation about your lies."

"We just want to go home, Harold." Carter said. He was worried Elodie would do something she would regret. She looked about ready to explode.

"We won't let you go until you tell us exactly what your parents did."

Jack was confused and tired of these questions. "*What* do you mean?"

Before Harold could answer, Elodie grabbed a tart from her basket and threw it at Harold's face. Harold was shocked. He wiped the strawberry goop off his face and glared at Elodie.

"Why you little..."

Elodie realised that she'd gone a bit too far. "Run!" she shouted to Carter and Jack.

They took off; Harold and his friends chased them.

Jack's lungs burned; his muscles ached. They finally got home and shut the gate. Harold stood on the other side of the gate prepared to end Elodie's life. Elodie stuck her tongue out at him from the other side.

"Ha!" she said. "You can't come in here, or else Mr Willows will murder you."

Harold growled and banged on the gate. Elodie yelped and ran inside with Jack and Carter trailing along behind her.

"You have some nerve, Elodie." said Jack, gasping. "But that was the most fun I had in days."

The three of them laughed as Thomas and Rogers came down the stairs, talking.

"I need someone to look over the piano, Rogers." Thomas said. "Mr Parker would like to buy it. I need someone to tune it. Do you know anyone?"

"I'm afraid I don't, sir," Rogers answered, "but I'll find someone."

"What about Tyler and Marie?" Elodie suggested.

Thomas and Rogers looked at her.

"They own *Anna's Place*, that music store downtown." Elodie explained. "Tyler can tune pianos."

"Oh, I see." Thomas said uncomfortably. "Rogers, will you please ask him to come to tune the piano? Tomorrow at noon."

Rogers said that he would and left to go ask them. Thomas looked at Jack, Elodie, and Carter suspiciously. Then, he went upstairs.

"Don't you ever think before saying something, Elodie?" Carter asked. "Tyler and Marie are Mr Willows' *parents*. He cast them out."

"I know, but maybe they'll make up if they're together again."

"Or they'll tear each other to bits." Jack said. "Why is he selling the piano anyway?"

Carter shrugged, "I guess we'll have to spend the rest of our time here," he said grinning, "since Harold boy is hunting us down outside."

Elodie and Jack smiled back at him. They spent the rest of the day exploring the house and climbing trees in the backyard. As Jack went to bed that night, he counted the days he would be there.

How was it possible that nearly a year had passed? He didn't want anything to do with this place last year. He wanted to return to his lonely, miserable life back home. Jack realised that he felt more at home in Springville than he did at his uncle and aunt's house. Elodie was right, as long as he was okay with the way he looked, nothing anybody said would matter to him.

18

There was a knock on the door. Elodie, Jack, and Carter rushed to open it. Three people were standing outside: Tyler, Marie and a man with grey hair and a fancy moustache.

"Hi!" Elodie cried, "You must be Mr Parker! Mr Willows said you would come to buy our piano. I love your moustache,"

Tyler and Marie tried not to laugh.

"Thank you, young lady," Mr Parker said with an amused smile. "You must be the famous Elodie."

Elodie nodded and told them to come in. She led Mr Parker to the living room where

Thomas was waiting. Jack and Carter led Tyler and Marie to the Music Room.

"How do you tune a piano anyway?" Jack asked once they got there.

"The answer to that question would take a very long explanation," Tyler said, sitting on the piano stool. "I think it's better if you just watch."

Marie started to play single keys on the piano. Elodie came into the room a few minutes later. Tyler opened the lid of the piano and examined the strings. Marie would play a note, and Tyler would adjust the strings. This went on for some time.

Jack, Elodie, and Carter watched curiously, even though they didn't understand anything. After half an hour, they got bored and started looking at the other instruments in the room. An hour later, Tyler and Marie had finished tuning the piano. They all left the music room and went upstairs to look for Thomas.

Thomas and Mr Parker were talking in the Living Room. Tyler and Marie walked in. Thomas locked eyes with Tyler for a minute and then greeted them. Tyler informed him that the piano was tuned. Thomas led Mr Parker upstairs, and

Tyler and Marie got ready to leave. Jack, Carter, and Elodie looked at each other. They had decided to admit to Tyler and Marie that they knew about Jane.

"We have to tell you something." Jack said. "We-we know about Jane. We saw her grave in the woods."

They told them everything they had found out. Marie and Tyler looked at each other in surprise.

"I see." Tyler said.

"We're sorry, Tyler." Elodie said. "We couldn't help finding out more."

"Do you think you can tell us anything about her?" Carter asked.

"I'm sorry, Carter." Marie said. "We promised to keep that a secret."

Tyler looked at their sad faces.

"How about we take a walk through the woods?" he suggested.

Everyone agreed.

They went to the backyard and entered the woods. They visited Jane's grave. Jack observed Tyler and Marie closely. Marie's eyes filled with tears, and Tyler put his arm around her.

"Well, I'm leaving the day after tomorrow." Jack said.

"Oh," Tyler said. "We'll come to see you off, Jack."

"You'll have to come to visit again," Marie said laughing, "or Elodie will deafen us with her complaining."

Elodie protested, and everyone laughed, except for Carter. He was squinting at something in the distance.

"What are those?" Carter asked.

They all looked at what he was pointing to. Amongst the trees were two arc-shaped objects. They were nearly impossible to see because they were covered in moss. Everyone walked towards them. They looked just like Jane's grave.

"More graves?" Elodie asked. She shivered.

Tyler looked confused, "I knew about Jane's grave, but whose are these?"

Elodie and Carter started to scrape off the moss. Only Tyler, Marie, and Jack recognized the names once they were visible.

In loving memory of

Richard Stanley

Beloved Son, Husband, and Father
July 29, 1904-November 8, 1943

In loving memory of

Anna Stanley

Beloved Daughter, Wife, and Mother
December 7, 1907-November 8, 1943

"Hey, Jack," Elodie said, with a spark of recognition, "isn't *your* last name Stanley?"

Jack didn't answer. He was breathing heavily. His parents; they were here. Suddenly he was blinded with rage. Tears filled his eyes as he ran past Tyler and Marie, and into the house. Carter and Elodie ran after him trying to stop him. Jack bumped into Ansley. She smiled at Jack but then saw his face.

"What's wrong?" she asked.

Jack pushed her away and ran upstairs. He burst into the Music Room where Mr Parker was playing the piano.

"Jack," Thomas said, "what is the meaning of-"

"Tell me!" Jack yelled.

Thomas and Mr Parker looked surprised. Elodie, Carter, and Ansley came into the room panting.

"Ansley," Thomas said, rubbing his forehead, "take him to his room."

"No!" Jack shouted, he fought Ansley's grip. "You have to tell me!"

Mr Parker stood, "Perhaps we can make final decisions on the instrument later, Thomas." he said. "I'll see myself out."

He smiled at Elodie and left.

"Just *what* do you think you're doing?" Thomas demanded. "You have humiliated me, Jack."

"Oh, leave the boy alone, Thomas," Marie said, coming into the room. "He saw his parents' graves in the forest."

The colour drained out of Thomas' face. "He did?"

"I think you owe him an explanation." Tyler said. "I think it's time you told the whole house the truth."

Thomas looked trapped. It was obvious that he didn't want to reveal his secret. Then he saw Jack's tear-streaked face and sighed in defeat.

"Ansley, gather everyone in the Living Room." Thomas said. "It's time I told you, my story."

* * *

Thomas, Elodie, Jack, Carter, Tyler, Marie, and the staff sat in the Living Room. Carter had offered to leave, but Jack had asked him to stay. He deserved to hear this as much as the rest of them did. Thomas looked like a scared little boy. Marie sat next to him and patted his hand.

"I-I haven't been honest with you." Thomas said. "You have been very faithful to me and my family for many years, it's time you know about my past and what I did. I have made many mistakes in my life. I understand completely if you would like to leave after hearing this."

Thomas turned to Jack, "You deserve to hear this the most, Jack. You've been living your life knowing only bits and pieces about your parents and their deaths. I promise you this explanation will help. Even if it does not answer all your questions, it will give you a few answers."

Thomas took a deep breath and began.

19

Once I started college, one of my closest friends, Jane Sasaki, left to study in Japan. We wrote to each other, and I slowly realised that I was in love with her. She returned two years later, and we got together. A few years later we got married. Life was good. I was the conductor of the local orchestra and Jane was a violinist.

We lived in this house. We led simple lives with easy schedules. Then, the war began. Germany took over Poland, Britain and France declared war. America managed to stay out of it until the Japanese attack on Pearl Harbour. The day after Pearl Harbour, America proclaimed war on Japan. That's when our problems started. Jane started to become very distant. She spent a lot of time by herself. She had received a job when she was in Japan. Usually, she wouldn't have much work. Jane would send a few letters back to her organisation and be done with it. After the Japanese attack, her work started to overflow.

Jane had to quit the orchestra to keep up with all her assignments and projects. She never properly told me what she was doing. She said that it was not important. One day, I was taking lunch up to the Study where Jane was working. I found her asleep with her desk covered in papers.

I set down the tray of food on the table when some writing on a piece of paper caught my eye. I picked up the letter and read over it. It was telling Jane to report whatever she had found out back to Japan. At first, I didn't understand what it said on the paper. Then, I thought about what was happening in the world. Japan and America were at war. If Japan was asking Jane to report back, then she must be a...

Jane woke up and saw my stunned expression. She demanded to know what I was doing and tried to take the piece of paper from me. I pulled it away from her and looked her in the eye."

"What is this, Jane?" I asked. "Why is Japan asking you to report back?"

"It's just something for my job." she said.

"It's time you tell me what your job is." I said. "Why are you reporting back to the Japanese? Are you a spy?"

I looked at her face, hoping to see something that told me I was wrong. But all I saw was guilt.

"How *could* you?" I yelled. "You are betraying your own country."

Jane glared at me, "*Japan* is my country, Thomas. I serve *Japan*."

"My rage exploded. We started yelling at each other. I criticised her for never telling me she was a spy and for accepting the job in the first place. Jane was begging at me to calm down. We stopped shouting at each other soon and didn't talk until the next day.

Jane told me that she swore an oath to secrecy as a spy and that she would not give up her job. She pleaded with me to keep all of this a secret."

I looked at her angrily, "I will, but don't expect me to forgive you for it."

I turned to leave the room. I didn't turn back, even when Jane started crying.

Over the next few days, Jane and I hardly spoke to each other. Jane tried to talk to me, but I would always end the conversation. I felt guilty for keeping a secret from my country. I knew I was helping a spy. I knew that I might be killed if someone found out. At that moment, I cared more about my own life than my wife's life.

Then, I made the biggest mistake of my life. I-I turned Jane in to the local police."

* * *

"You did *what?*" Elodie asked.

Thomas looked at his hands shamefully. Everyone looked at Thomas in surprise.

"But she was your *wife*." Elodie continued.

"Hush, Elodie." Marie said. She took her son's hand, "Go on."

* * *

I called the police station and told them everything. Jane was visiting Anna, Jack's mother. She said that she wanted to leave her violin with her, just in case. When she returned, I couldn't look at her. She asked what was wrong, but before I could answer, there was a knock on the door. Jane was about to open it when four police officers stormed inside.

They looked at Jane and immediately knew that she was the Japanese spy I told them about. They grabbed her arms and said that she was under arrest. Jane was confused at first, but then she realized what was happening. She looked at me, her eyes were full of fury. She looked like she was going to attack me, but then her face crumpled."

Jane's eyes filled with tears, "I thought you loved me."

Those were the last words she said before the police took her away. After they left, I broke down.

Days passed, but I hardly noticed it. The local police informed me that Jane had been taken to an internment camp in Topaz. I didn't talk to anyone for weeks. Every morning, I expected to hear Jane call me for breakfast. Her voice seemed to echo around the house. I wanted to feel proud of myself. I had done my country a favour, hadn't I? But all I felt was guilt. I took a break from the orchestra and filled my time with studying for my PhD.

My friends clearly saw that something was wrong, but I never told them what. No matter how many times they asked.

One day, I was in the Music Room. I hadn't gone in there for weeks. I looked at my old cello; it begged to be played. I tried to make some music, but my arms wouldn't work. That's when I noticed an envelope on Jane's piano. I put the cello aside and opened the envelope. It was a letter from Jane. I don't know when she wrote it, but it seemed that she knew she would be arrested soon.

I read the letter.

My dearest Thomas,

It is my hope that you never have to read this letter, but if you do, I suppose you know everything now. Something has probably happened to me. Please forgive me for not telling you, I took an oath that I would tell no one. Please do not blame yourself if I die. I assure you it was not your fault. We are all destined to die. Life is only special because it ends. Live your life to the fullest.

Love,

Jane

Tears pricked my eyes after I read the letter. I had to apologize to her. I decided to send Jane a letter. I didn't know whether it would reach the Japanese internment camp, but I had to try. I went to my Study and started to write a letter to Jane.

My Dear Jane,

My days are filled with grief for you. I realize my horrible mistake now that you are gone. I know it will be very hard for you, but please forgive me. My pride blinded me from seeing how much I love you. I will make-

Suddenly, I heard Jane's laughter around me. I knew it wasn't enough to just write a letter to her. I needed to bring her back here. I needed to show her that I still loved her. I don't know what I was thinking. Perhaps my sorrow blocked my good sense. I knew that Jane would not return home unless I brought her back. So, I decided to break into the Japanese internment camp and bring her back.

I spent a few days planning how I was going to get Jane back. She was being kept in Topaz which took about two hours to get to by bus. I didn't know what condition she would be in, so we needed somewhere to recover. I planned my break-in, our escape, and our supply list. I was ready. Or at least I thought so. I had no idea what I was walking into.

I took the bus to Topaz and found the internment camp. There were thousands of people there. Children ran around the place while adults talked to each other with grim expressions. How was I going to find Jane? I stayed hidden for a while and observed the place. Police would patrol around the area, but there was a small window of time when they would change their positions. At that moment, I quickly hurried to the barbed fence and called to a young woman playing with her child.

She cautiously came over to me.

"Do you know a woman named Jane Sasaki Willows?" I asked.

The woman thought for a while, "I think so. She was brought here a few weeks ago,"

"Is she being watched?" I asked.

"All of us are being watched, sir," the woman told me, "The guards were told to shoot anyone who tried to escape."

"If possible, can you please tell Jane to come here after dark?" I asked. "It's very important."

The woman hesitated, but then she nodded.

"Thank you," I said and hurried back to my hiding place.

I waited a few hours, devising a plan on how to get Jane out of there. Barbed wire fences surrounded the camp, and the main gates were always guarded. My only chance was those few minutes when the guards switched their posts. I quickly went to our meeting spot when the guards weren't there and dug into the loose dirt. It was a miracle that no one noticed the hole in the ground once I finished.

Around midnight, I saw someone lurking around the hole. I ran to it and saw Jane. She looked horrible. Her face was pale, and she had gotten extremely thin. Her cheeks were sunken, and her eyes looked feverish.

Jane's eyes widened when she saw me."

"Thomas?" she said. "What're you doing here?"

"Jane, I'm so sorry." I said. "I've come to make things right. I gestured to the hole that went under the barbed fence. "We're going home."

It took Jane a second to understand what I said. She shook her head, "No. I will not break out of this place. It would put both of us in danger."

"If you aren't coming with me, I'm staying," I said stubbornly.

At that moment, a guard came to his post and saw us.

"Hey!" he yelled, "What're you doing?"

"Come on, Jane." I said urgently.

Jane wavered, then climbed through the hole. We started to run. The guard yelled and then blew his whistle. We heard shouts as we ran through the dark desert. The guards started to shoot at us, but we kept running. We were so close to the hiding spot I had made, then Jane suddenly fell. I thought she tripped, but then I saw a pool of blood form at her side."

"Jane!" I called.

I ran to her and picked her up. I carried her to the small cave I had found. It was nearly impossible to find in the dark.

"Jane!" I whispered. I gently slapped her cheek.

Her eyes fluttered open. She saw me and gripped my hand.

"Thomas," she croaked, "you have to go. They'll kill you if they find you here with me,"

I shook my head, "I'm not leaving you,"

She smiled sadly at me, "I-I'm not going to make it." she clutched her side.

Her dress was soaked in blood.

Tears filled my eyes, and I wiped them furiously. I didn't want to accept it, but I knew that Jane was right. We would never make it out without being caught."

"Please go," Jane pleaded, "you must leave me here. I'll always be with you, and we will see each other again, someday."

I bent down and kissed her cheek. I held her hand until her eyes closed, and her muscles relaxed. Then, I took off my bloodied jacket and laid it over her.

I looked at Jane for the last time and ran out of the cave. I didn't stop running until I got to the bus station. It was dawn by then. I bought a train ticket and returned to Springville. I went home and threw my clothes away. My parents weren't home, thank goodness. I washed my face and went to visit my friends, Anna and Richard.

I must've looked like I hadn't slept all night because Richard immediately took me in and gave me something to eat. I tried to tell him something, but he wouldn't let me until I ate and calmed down. Anna came and joined us."

"I made so many mistakes, Richard." I blubbered. "I didn't mean to."

Richard just patted my back and told me to settle down. Once I finished eating, I took a deep breath. I was about to tell them what happened last night when there was a banging on the door.

Anna hurried to open it and police officers stormed in.

"What is the meaning of this?" Richard cried.

"Mr Stanley, I understand that you were good friends with Jane Sasaki Willows?" an officer asked him.

Richard nodded.

"Last night there was a break-in at the Topaz Japanese Internment camp. Mrs Willows managed to escape with another person. We found her corpse in a cave a few hours later. We just searched Mr Willows' house, but we didn't find anything suspicious." the officer said.

"You had no right!" I cried.

"I am a police officer, Mr Willows. It is my job to do these things. We will have to search this house as well."

We couldn't do anything to stop them. They turned the place upside down. One police officer went upstairs and came rushing down with a violin case. My stomach lurched. It belonged to Jane; her name was engraved onto a leather patch on the lid of the case.

The head officer raised his eyebrows. He opened the case and examined the violin.

"That doesn't belong to you!" Anna cried.

The officer ignored her. He carefully picked up the violin and looked at it while his associates searched the case. I thought he was done, but then he pulled out a pocket knife and pressed it to the centre bout of the instrument. It popped out. He cut the rest of it. Inside the violin were several papers, all in Japanese.

The officer smiled triumphantly.

"Mr and Mrs Stanley, you are both under arrest for treason." he said.

The police officers grabbed their hands and dragged them outside. I tried to say something, but my voice wouldn't work. Anna and Richard fought. Richard kicked the guard who was taking Anna away. The head officer looked bored, he pulled out his revolver and shot Richard. Anna screamed. She fought the officers and crouched down to where Richard lay.

She sobbed. I watched helplessly. I should've admitted that I was the one who broke into the camp, but I only watched. Anna shouted at the officer in rage. She lunged at him, and he shot her as well. I was so shocked I couldn't move."

"Take them away." the head officer said.

They all left. I never saw Richard or Anna again. I received a call a few hours later informing me that both of them had died. I could've done something, *anything*, to stop their deaths, but I didn't

That day, my wife and my two best friends died. It was all my fault.

20

Everyone sat in the Living Room so stunned they couldn't even move. Ansley hugged a pillow to her chest, Theo sat next to her, looking lost, and Marta and Rogers stared at the ground. Elodie was sitting on the floor in front of Tyler. She was leaning against his legs sniffling. Carter sat next to her, looking fiercely at the floor, as though he could change the past if he stared hard enough.

Tyler stroked Elodie's hair and looked at Thomas and Marie. Marie was crying softly. Jack sat in an armchair next to Tyler. He observed Thomas. Thomas had his head in his hands. Jack could see tears flowing down his face. Jack didn't know what to think. Thomas was responsible for his parents' deaths.

Everyone was so lost that they didn't see a figure lurking at the window, listening to everything.

* * *

For a few minutes, they all sat silently. Elodie recovered soon and looked at Thomas.

"Mr Willows, you have to tell people what really happened." Elodie said. "Someone spread a rumour about Jack. I understand now. They've been calling him a spy because everyone thinks that his parents helped a Japanese spy."

Thomas looked at Elodie helplessly. He looked like a boy. "I know." he whispered.

Jack was about to say something when there was a rustling at the window. He looked at it and saw someone run away.

"Oh no." he said.

"That was Harold Peters!" Elodie cried. "He'll tell everyone what he's found out."

She hurried out the door and chased him.

"Harold!" she cried. "Harold, stop!"

Harold ran down the street and through an alley. Elodie ran after him.

"Please, Harold!" Elodie called. "Stop!"

Harold stopped at a small bridge. He went over to the ledge and looked at the water below. Elodie went to join him. He looked at her. Elodie's eyes widened in shock. Harold was crying.

"What's wrong?" she asked.

"I'm sorry, Elodie." Harold said. "I promise I won't tell anyone what I heard."

Elodie was confused. "What were you doing there anyway?"

Harold took a deep breath, "My mother died during Pearl Harbour. My father was furious at the Japanese. He heard about Jack's parents, and he was determined to get revenge on someone. He made me find out more about Jack, but now that I heard that story..."

Elodie cautiously patted his arm. "I'm sorry about your mother, Harold. I know it must be hard for you. I promise Mr Willows will make things right. Just don't tell anyone before he does."

Harold nodded and then laughed. He wiped his tears, "You better not tell anyone that I cried."

Elodie smiled, "I can't promise that."

* * *

Elodie returned home and assured everyone that Harold wouldn't reveal anything to anyone. Marta had made everyone tea, but Thomas wouldn't have any.

"Thomas told Tyler and me that he was going to keep this whole affair a secret." Marie said. "We were furious and left him. We took over Anna's Place, your mother's music store, Jack."

"The only person I told was your uncle and aunt," Thomas said.

They sat in silence for a while. Then, Jack stood up.

"You made a lot of mistakes, Uncle Thomas," Jack started, "it was wrong of you to break into the Japanese camp. It was wrong of you to turn in your wife. You kept all of this a secret. Your mistakes led to Jane's death and my parents' deaths."

Thomas looked down in shame. "I'm sorry, Jack."

"But now that I heard your story, I see that you did everything out of love." Jack said. "You loved Jane, and you loved my parents. I know this may sound strange, but I understand why you made these mistakes."

Everyone looked at Jack in amazement.

"Once in church, the preacher said that our lives are planned out. There's nothing we can do about it. We are born at a certain time, and we die at a certain time. I don't think anything could've stopped Jane's death, or my parent's death." Jack took a breath, "So many people would not have been in my life if it weren't for you, Uncle Thomas."

He wanted to hate Thomas for what he did. He was the reason he was an orphan, after all. But now that he saw Thomas for who he really was, a man who'd lost his wife and friends but stayed strong the whole time, all Jack felt was love.

"I love you, Uncle Thomas," Jack said.

Thomas' eyes filled with tears, but he smiled, "I promise you, Jack. I will make things right."

They spent the rest of the day talking. Elodie, Jack, and Carter had finally finished their investigation. Tyler talked to Thomas for a long time. Marie, Theo, Ansley, and Rogers helped Marta in the kitchen.

Jack sat and thought for a while. The truth was very painful, but knowing it gave him some clarity about this life. He watched Elodie and Carter argue about who was a better detective.

Jack smiled. He really had the best of friends.

21

That night, Jack lay in his bed unable to sleep. His things were scattered across the room. Jack stared out the window and looked around the room. His eyes rested on his desk where Jane's journal and the box with the marriage certificates were. Jack got up and went to his desk.

He decided to return them.

Jack tiptoed out of his room and walked to Thomas' room. He knocked on the door.

"Come in." Thomas called.

Jack went in. Thomas smiled at him.

"Hello, Jack."

"Hi, Uncle Thomas." Jack said. "I just wanted to give these back to you."

He put the journal and box on Thomas' bed. Thomas thanked him. Jack was about to leave when Thomas stopped him.

"Wait, Jack," he said, "I need to apologise to you."

"What for?" Jack asked.

"Everything. I've been very rude to you ever since you got here. It's just that you remind me so much of your father. I see him every time I look at you."

"Really?" Jack whispered.

Thomas nodded and gestured for Jack to sit on the bed.

"Your father loved to read, and he was also a violinist." Thomas said. "He was also a luthier. You got that scar while playing with one of his unfinished violins."

Jack listened eagerly. No one had ever talked to him about his father.

"Your parents, Jane, and I loved to play quartets together." Thomas explained. "Jane's favourite song was *Oh My Love Is Like A Red Red Rose*. That's why I stormed out like that on my birthday. The song reminded me of her. Your mother was the kindest person I've ever met. She was ever so gentle; it drove the rest of us mad."

They stayed up late, talking.

I may have lost my parents, Jack thought as Thomas told him stories, *But I still have a family.*

22

Carter coughed as dust filled his nose.

"What are we doing here, Elodie?" he asked. "We should be with Jack right now; he's leaving in twenty minutes!"

"We *need* to give him a present before he leaves." Elodie said. "I have the perfect one. I remember seeing it here."

"Why would the perfect present be in the attic?" Carter asked.

"*I don't know*, ok?" Elodie said. "Just look."

Meanwhile, Jack was waiting for his aunt and uncle outside. Tyler, Marie, the staff, and Thomas were with him, but where were Elodie and Carter?

Thomas put a hand on Jack's shoulder and smiled at him. Jack smiled back. The day had been filled with farewells and presents. Tyler and Marie had given him a music book. Ansley gave him a journal and Marta gave him the recipe for her scrambled eggs.

"So you can remember the taste of my food." Marta said.

Thomas had found an old picture of Jack's parents and gave it to him.

Soon, a carriage drove up the street and stopped at the main gate. Jack's uncle and aunt stepped out of it and greeted everyone. Thomas explained that Jack knew everything and that he was going to clear Anna and Richard's names. They seemed a bit surprised at this, but Jack could tell that they were grateful.

Thomas put Jack's suitcase inside the carriage. Jack hugged everyone and bid them farewell. He didn't want to leave without seeing Carter and Elodie. Jack looked at the house, hoping to see them. When he didn't, Jack sadly started to climb into the carriage.

"Jack! Wait!" Elodie called. She was running to him. Carter followed, holding a violin case.

They stopped in front of Jack, panting.

"We didn't want you to leave without anything to remember us by." Elodie said.

Carter handed him the violin case. It had the name *Richard* engraved on it, "It was your father's." he said. "It belongs to you now."

Jack looked at his friends. His eyes filled with tears, and he threw his arms around them.

"Thank you," he said. "I'm going to miss you very much."

Carter and Elodie hugged him back.

"Goodbye, then." Jack said, wiping his nose.

"Hey, friends don't say goodbye, Jack," Elodie said, "they say 'see you again'."

Jack smiled. He was about to enter the carriage again when someone called to him.

"Wait!" It was Harold Peters.

Harold ran to Jack, "I wanted to apologise for everything I did."

"That's alright, Harold." Jack said.

Harold gave him a toothy grin and handed him a basket, "Strawberry tarts."

Jack accepted it gratefully. He climbed into the carriage and looked at all of them one more time.

"Visit soon, Jack." Thomas said.

Jack nodded. The carriage started and Jack waved to everyone. He didn't stop until he couldn't see them anymore.

23

Springville, Utah
1943

Thomas sat in Anna's Place with his head in his hands. What had he done? Jane, Richard, and Anna were dead. Guilt seemed to weigh him down. Then, Thomas felt someone tap on his knee. A two-year-old boy toddled up to him. He had a long scar across his left cheek.

"Papa?" he asked, tugging on Thomas' pants.

Thomas picked the boy up and set him on his lap, "No, Jack," Thomas said, "not papa. Uncle Thomas."

Jack rubbed his eyes sleepily. He started to cry. "Mama?"

Thomas rocked him gently and went to the kitchen. He gave Jack a bottle. Jack immediately took it from him and started drinking the milk. Thomas looked at him sadly. Jack didn't understand that he was an orphan. He didn't understand that his parents were dead because of Thomas.

Thomas couldn't help it.

Tears started to flow down his cheeks, "I'm so sorry, Jack."

Jack looked at Thomas curiously. He wiped the tears off his face.

Thomas smiled and kissed his hand. "You're a sweet boy." he said.

Thomas took care of Jack for the rest of the day. He called Richard's brother and told him what had happened. Richard's brother said that they would come there as soon as possible. Jack was oblivious to it all. He played with Thomas.

He went into the music store and banged on the piano.

Thomas laughed, "You'll be a great musician someday, Jack. Just like your parents."

Thomas crouched down in front of Jack, "I promise you, Jack. Someday, I'll tell you what happened to your parents. I'll make everything right. You'll know the truth."

Thomas tapped Jack's nose, and Jack laughed. His laughter sounded like music.

Acknowledgments

A very special thanks to Shawna Fiscus and Uncle Joel Alba for taking the time to edit this book.

Thank you to my English teacher, Amy Brown, who encouraged me to write.

I would like to send lots of love to my family. To my sister, Emily, the first one to read this book. To my mother for always supporting me.

Thanks to Susan for a beautiful cover.

Finally, I wouldn't have written this story without my incredible father. Thank you for helping me through every step of the journey.